A Good Man

Edward Docx was born in 1972 and lives in London. He is the author of *The Calligrapher* and *Self Help*, winner of the Geoffrey Faber Memorial Award and longlisted for the 2007 Man Booker Prize.

Also by Edward Docx

The Calligrapher
Self Help

A Good Man

EDWARD DOCX

PICADOR SHOTS

First published 2008 by Picador
an imprint of Pan Macmillan Ltd
Pan Macmillan, 20 New Wharf Road, London N1 9RR
Basingstoke and Oxford
Associated companies throughout the world
www.panmacmillan.com

ISBN 978-0-330-46097-2

1 3 5 7 9 8 6 4 2

A CIP catalogue record for this book is available from
the British Library.

Printed and bound in the UK by
CPI Mackays, Chatham ME5 8TD

Visit www.picador.com to read more about all our books
and to buy them. You will also find features, author interviews and
news of any author events, and you can sign up for e-newsletters
so that you're always first to hear about our new releases.

Contents

❧

I

Hook-fingered and with clumsy mitten grip, he gropes his way. Veins of ice luminous in the fissures of the rock. The wind is at full roar. Deafens him. Blinds the white light of his head torch in furious flurries. He has no axe. He will be blown to his death if he does not slide to it. Ten years since last he passed this way. Seldom in darkness. Never in a storm.

He can no longer be sure if he is following the wall of his ravine or perhaps a smaller cleft that leads off. He kicks his boots into the snow, trying to find footholds on the ice beneath. Twice, three times, he has almost fallen. A rock comes loose, hits hard against his knee. He cannot hear his own curses. This is too steep. Wrong. Shards sheer as he struggles for holds. He edges sideways. Another rock wall to his left. He reaches for it. Slips. Hangs on. Conscious of his human weight on the slope. Surely he is climbing the mountain itself, not the low saddle of the ridge. The wind is whipping the spindrift, so that the snow seems more to rise than to fall. His hands are stiffening, cold. His mittens saturated. He must up.

Maddened, he scrambles and struggles, almost on all fours. Slithers back. Makes only a third of the distance that his effort seeks. Tries to stand. Paws once more at the rock wall on his left. Scrambles again. Almost to his feet. His boots skidding, then digging in, skidding, then digging in. Trying to cheat the mountain by going too quickly to be caught. Heart like a fist.

The defile seems to be narrowing further. Rock pressing in. A bank of ice, glistening crazily in his torchlight. Blocking his way. He pushes up, through. Burrowing. Clawing.

Abruptly, there is no more.

But he does not dare to stand for fear of the

wind's strength. So now he hauls himself sideways across the flat. His lamp a pale and meagre cone, lighting only the swirl and churn six thick inches from his face. The covering is thinner here. And he feels the rock tearing at his thigh as he scrapes across. Ten paces. Twenty. Then the ground gives way. He swings about so that his feet are first. Half sits. Paddles at the snow with his mittens. Urges himself over the edge. Into the glissade. Into the fall. Starts to slide. Is falling.

Now he careers downwards on his back, the snow streaming towards him, fleeting glimpses of black rock and the baneful glint of ice. No longer caring whether he is in the right gully for his descent or about to plunge over some frozen waterfall. Half the time seeming desperately to be slowing himself – sitting up, shoving in the heels of hands through his mittens, the heel of his boots. Half the time seeming to be pushing himself forward, trying to get his body to slide further on his oilskin. The fall sharpens. He is kicking, scuffing,

3

his light jerking, bouncing, then knocked out, then ripped from his head. In the darkness, he is only his breathing and his muffled cries. His boots pound into solid rock and he kicks against it to spin away. His body is skewed around and sliding sideways too fast, his arm outstretched ahead. He tries to correct the fall with his other boot. But he can get no purchase. Bones and hide.

He lies awhile. Icy water welling through his clothes. He opens his eyes but it makes no difference. He can see nothing. The wind is no longer howling though. And after the violence of his fall, the snow seems absurdly gentle as it settles on his cheek. The leeward side of the mountain.

There is rock behind him. His back, he thinks, has been saved by his pack. His heart is slowing. His head does not hurt. He is alive.

He twists out of the straps of his pack. Then he bites off his mitten – the taste of the wet earth – and feels his way along the zips and fastenings.

Eventually his frozen fingers find the shape he seeks. Deep inside, bedded in the softness of his clothes, is his second lamp.

The light is a miracle.

He is lying in a small stream. Disbelieving, he raises himself. His knee is painful but takes his weight.

He can see twenty paces where the stream runs down a shallow gorge. Scree, boulders, flitches of frozen fern. He is just above the snowline. He fastens the new lamp on his head and lifts his pack. Heavier with the wet. His boots two rag-stuffed ice buckets. He steps forward carefully. He follows the water. He thinks the snow is thinning to rain.

Two hours. Then, at last, he rounds the corner of the track. Sodden. And there, stops still.

II

The house in the fold of the mountain stands unchanged. A single light burning. He takes off and extinguishes his lamp. Begins gradually to make out the shape of the barn, the sheds, the low-walled garden . . . Surely, he has lived only in his coming and going from this place; all since, the bitter necessity of the years required to preserve himself for this return. A jagged convulsion in his throat. His body wanting to weep. The rain running down his face.

He should not be here. He has not been able to imagine himself here, has not dared to do so. And the enormity of his trespass continues to stall him, though the cold is tightening. But that light is also the light of her sickness and at last he thumbs his slick hair from his forehead and begins to walk towards the house.

For the first time he thinks of her girl. If Pavel is

unable to rise, as her boy said, then perhaps it will be her girl who opens the door. He has never met her girl. She was not born. This valley is most likely among the safest places in the country – cut off, save by boat, from even the small town, mercifully unmapped and mostly unknown except by those round about. And there are no strangers here. Not yet. But even so, he must take care to quell her fears immediately. He has no idea of the hour. It is dark so long in the winter.

The rain is moving again, squalling in from the sea. The barn looms above him and he passes by, feeling the clog of his boots in the mud. He lifts the sticking gate and pushes it open in one familiar movement. Clenches his lamp in his hand. He hopes that the girl will not look like her mother.

He does not know whether to knock softly or with great force. Some part of him has been hoping he would perish. He balls his fist and thuds the heel of his hand against the door. His heart twice the volume.

Again.

A light above. The window opening.

He squints into the icy rain. A man's face he can hardly see. Pavel.

He shouts up: Hello. I have brought you medicine. For your wife. For you. Your boy arrived late this morning. I came straight.

You've come from the village?

Straight.

The rain streaming in his eyes. The sky the sea.

Your boat? Have you a boat?

I walked around by the coast. No boats are putting out. But the doctor said it was better tonight. I . . . I said I would walk.

Wait.

The window shuts. He bows his head. He has been disguising his voice. He should have said his name.

The light from within is strong. The girl is no more than nine. She has one eye shut with sleep; her hair is wild, red and gold, a dozen hues in between. Her pullover reaches to her knees – blue and green hoops. She is barefoot. He thinks it a second miracle that the world is coloured after all. He thinks also that he must appear filthy and ragged.

He looks away, somewhere above her head. Gently he says: Hello. I have brought medicine for your mother.

I know.

Wait a minute. He swings off the pack.

Do you want to come in the kitchen?

He hesitates.

No. My boots.

But he takes a step into the little entrance hall because it is absurd to remain outside.

Everything is instantly familiar. Ten years – of no consequence. The same narrow wooden stair behind. He undoes his pack and reaches in, one hand holding the door open behind him. Rain falling across the threshold when the wind blows it so.

Here.

Thank you.

She clutches it to her chest, leaves him standing and runs directly up the stairs, fast as she can.

He does not know whether to move properly inside or stand out. And it takes some strength to hold the door steadily ajar and so prevent the wind throwing it open or slamming it closed. Voices. His ears straining. The girl running back.

My father says thank you and sorry that he cannot come down and that you can sleep in the den and do you need new clothes? The bed is made ready and it's dry. I have to show you. Do you want bread and honey? You can have some.

No. Thank you. Not now. You should go back to sleep.

Tomorrow then. We have special honey. Already she is pulling on her boots.

He thinks she should wear socks and that her feet will surely be hurt by the roughness.

She does not bother to lace them properly.

He thinks she will trip in the darkness.

She opens the door to the kitchen and returns with a torch.

He follows her down the wet stone path. She holds her coat over her head against the rain. Her light bright. Nothing ever locked. Here the directives do not reach. Not yet.

In she goes. He follows. Past a jumble of furniture and boxes to a clear space at the far end of the cabin. A table. A chair. A chest of drawers. A bed by the window, so beautifully made that he cannot look at it and must instead examine the shelf – empty jars and a broken clock.

Here. She gives him the torch.

Thank you. He is conscious of the mud on his boots, his clothes, his hands.

There are piles of blankets, she says. She indicates the chest.

Rain like fingertips drumming on the roof. Nails when the wind hardens.

She stands watching.

I'll be all right. Thank you.

She stands watching.

I have dry clothes and I'll be plenty warm enough.

She nods. There's a lamp if you want to light it. It's paraffin. Or hang the torch on the hook.

He realizes that it is her intention to go back in the dark. No, he says. I'll come with you so you can see the way.

I know the way. A smile.

His pack falls over where he has stood it up.

Thank you, he says again.

Thank you, too.

She raises her coat above her head. He follows her out, trying to shine the torch ahead of her, though she is in front.

What's your name?

Anna Pavlovna. What is yours?

He tells her his name.

III

He stirs with the first of the light. And for a moment he is bewildered – not knowing himself. Then his memory awakes and takes possession once more. He is sore. He has not slept in the bed for shame of his state but lain on the top, covered in loose blankets. He raises himself, stands. His knee a searing pain. His pack is propped against the leg of the table. He thinks of the bottle inside. The cabin smells of damp wood and the window above the table is wet with condensation. He rubs at the glass. He can see the track along which he has come, between the fields, past the barn, the valley narrowing, the snow line wintry low. He cannot see the house.

The sheer fact of the day is incredible to him. Neither can he believe that he is here, in this place again. Quickly, he strips off his underclothes. Drapes himself in a blanket. He must wash.

By the door, chairs are piled on one another. Rows of boots. A camp-bed. A table. An old lamp. A box marked 'gloves', another one 'socks'. A third: 'baby clothes'. It is not her hand. He does not remember having even looked in here before. Perhaps it had not been fixed up back then. Before the children there was no requirement.

Outside, the silent magnificence of the world stills him. The clouds lie at half the greater mountains' height. Mist drifts and sits and drifts again. Rocky crags, shadowy ridges, hanging fields of ice and snow, revealed and concealed.

The wind has abated.

He walks over the little hump of land, down the mossy path between the bowed brown reeds, away from the house. By the river, he removes the rest of his clothes. Folds the blanket on top. Then, feet awkward on the stones, he runs as best and fast as he can into the water. Breathless with the shock. Submerges himself. Up, gasping. Throws back his head to keep the water from his eyes. Bones hurting. Counts to ten, rubs himself, splashes, makes five, then dips again. Struggles out, shivering.

He regrets the use of the blanket as a makeshift towel and hangs it across the legs of the upturned chairs by the doors. He would prefer it if every moment of his existence could be ravelled up behind him. He pulls a shirt from his pack. The fact of his carrying a change of clothes betrays his intentions. And so he flinches as he dresses, not dry enough to do so. Bruised and scratched and scraped and cut. He resolves against himself to go, immediately. Resolves to stay. A day. A night. A day and a night, no more. Resolves to stay. Resolves to go.

Someone knocking.

He calls out hello.

The girl enters. He pulls on his oatmeal woollen jumper from the pack. She shuts the door with a gentle kick behind her. She is carrying a tray. She is dressed in her hoops.

I made you some porridge, she says. Be careful though. It is hot. She places the tray on the table by the window. This is the honey. There is bread.

Thank you.

The tea is hot, too. The milk is fresh though — if you want it on its own.

He stands awkwardly by the bed.

Did you see the lightning?

He hesitates. No, I didn't.

She is confused.

You could see the waves lit up — all white with frosty hats. They were like mountains. My father says you came around by the sea.

He has no answer. He has lied because he thinks the truth of his coming over the ridge might betray his eagerness. His recklessness. And so now he has to lie again. This is how it always is.

I was concentrating on the path. It was difficult.

But the girl does not seem to mind or care.

Don't let your porridge go cold, she says. It is horrible when it goes cold. I hate it.

She makes a face just like her mother and so he sits and begins to eat so that he doesn't have to look at her.

Silence save for his spoon.

Condensation runs down the window.

The latch on the door.

He looks around the other way – Pavel. He is dressed in a dark full-length coat, fur on his shoulders. Two steps and already he can hear the labour of the man's breathing.

Pavel nods, halts, speaks in shallow gasps to his daughter: Go back in. Mind your mother for me now.

The girl has been standing by the bed, watching him all the while. He turns to her and raises his spoon.

Thank you for bringing this, Anna, he says.

Thank you for bringing the medicine, she replies.

Then she goes, making a show of shutting the door carefully.

Pavel eases himself down onto the bed. Eat, he says. Please.

Thank you.

But his appetite has fled incredulous and the bowl is cooling. All the same, he forces himself to mouth what remains, thankful that the chair at the table allows him to keep his back to the room. Rain is falling again. He thinks his life is surely impossible. For even if every turn were wrong, surely he could not have found himself here, now, in this cabin, with this man.

Pavel seems to concentrate on composing his breath.

He forces himself to swallow.

Thank you for your help, Pavel says at last.

It's nothing.

The sound of his spoon.

Why did you come here?

The boy said she was ill and the doctor said—

Why were you even in the village? Why did you leave the capital? Why are you here?

He hates the milk, sips it all the same.

I brought you the medicine, he says.

For your own reasons. Pavel tenses against a cough.

To save her life.

Her life was not in danger.

The doctor said pneumonia. You are both in danger.

I sent the boy. He would have been back today if you had not come.

And I was there when the boy arrived. I came straight.

Why were you there? It is three days from the capital. Why?

He turns and looks at her husband. Long narrow nose. Clean shaven even now. Too tall for her. Pale blue eyes. Yet he finds he can see Pavel for an instant only, and then not at all; rather he scans the man's features as if he might read her thoughts there reflected. As if looking at some cast where-upon she pressed her wishes.

I wanted to see her again before I died.

You cannot see her. The other shakes his head slowly. And you are not dying.

He drinks the tea.

Pavel speaks into the silence: She does not know that it is you.

Then do not tell her it is me. He straightens. Pavel, forgive me, but you should not be out of your bed. And you will be days recovering yet. I am here and fit. Let me work for you. I'm sure there are a hundred tasks you need doing. Give me the most pressing. And I will leave tomorrow, as your son returns. You will not see me again.

The other watches him with steady eyes.

The tea is the only thing he likes. And he drinks it eagerly now, as if to vouch for his own integrity.

The doctor says penicillin is a wonder cure. But it's not instant. Let me help you. Let me work a day. Tell me what you need me to do. This place cannot be left a week. Go back to her. Care for her. Let me do your work.

Pavel regards him a while longer. Breathes in and out. A sheen of sweat on his pale temple. No expression on his face. At length he says: I have buried the grain and I have hidden the wood. In case . . . in case they came. We need to move some of the wood now. You have brought the winter. I will have Anna show you where.

I understand. He bows his head. Thank you, he says.

But I will not tell her that you are here. You leave tomorrow.

I leave tomorrow.

IV

The rain falls most of the day. The wind flattens his wet clothes against his skin but he pays it little heed. Cart by cart, he loads the wood, drags it from the trees down the path half-hidden beneath the melting snow, drags it the quarter-mile to the main track, drags it to the woodshed and piles it carefully, large and medium and small. Warm with the work. No rest, no thought.

Her girl comes out with soup. He drinks it down in the doorway of the barn, listening to the rain and looking down the track that leads to the sea.

He rises straight and begins again. The mud deepening. The wheels sticking. His boots caked and filthy, thick-soled with the clinging earth. His hands beginning to blister with the roughness of the handle. Glad that they do so. One cart after another. Head bowed. Trying not to glance up at the house on each return.

Towards the end of the day, the rain thins and the girl reappears and gives him further instructions. He sets off for the shore directly, past the returning goats, to where Pavel's fishing boat is dragged high.

He stops before the sea. The light is seeping from the sky. The waves almost the colour of slate. Salt on his lips. Stinging in his cuts. Hands red, splintered and cold. The coastal path winds up to his left, disappears over the brow, reappears a dark grey thread, then cuts back and forth in just visible scars across the black-faced cliff.

On that path he kissed her for the first time. Held her body against his. There was so much desire. And yet – a madness this – no trust anywhere but in their bed. As though their bodies were pledged by some sure and binding contract that their conscious selves could never discover.

He stands too long in these recollections and the day is ghosting before he sees the boat again, the incoming tide. He hobbles across the rocks. With numb fingers, he struggles to open the rusted catch of the boathouse. More of Pavel's winter stores. He fills the bucket with salted fish from the bin. Carries it back at a slow lope, the sea-birds crying overhead.

The track is three fields long. Then the cross of stones, then the gate, then the house. Everything as it always was. Nothing changed, save in him, save in her. He goes around. Sets the bucket by the door. Stays a moment. Holds his heavy breath. Listens. Knocks hard. Walks quickly away.

He washes himself in the stream again, his torch balanced on the rock casting an eerie glow on the water black as bitumen.

Then he waits.

An hour passes. He must surely leave. He has no sense of what he is doing, neither what he hopes for, nor fears. He sits alone on the bed. His day is over. The paraffin lamp gives off its smoky light.

He is dressed in his last shirt, dry underclothes, his oatmeal sweater. But he is shivering still from the icy water in the stream. He thinks perhaps he is sickening. His forehead feels hot and yet he is cold in his bones. He holds his head in his hands. Imagines himself a thirty-year servant of the family. Imagines himself their killer. Imagines himself their saviour. The temperature is falling. The sky will be full of stars.

It is not the girl's knock.

I have bought you some stew. Anna made it for you. It's hot. There are potatoes.

Thank you.

Here.

He rises, steps towards Pavel and accepts the tray.

Can I sit on the bed?

Pavel, this is your house.

Thank you.

The sweat has gone but Pavel continues to

move with great care as if wary that the slightest strain will lead to a fit.

The stew is some kind of Ukha and tastes of onion and fish. It occurs to him that they have made it especially. He eats square on at the little table. He is careful with the bones.

You are mending, Pavel? He speaks half over his shoulder.

It is true what they say – penicillin is the wonder cure.

All the same, you should not be up from your bed.

Pavel breathes awhile. Then without changing his voice he asks: How long before there is collective in the village?

I do not know.

They take everything?

Yes. There are impossible quotas.

I have heard this. Set by officials?

The Central Committee set them.

Dear God.

People are dying all over the country, Pavel. Meanwhile we are to read that the people's government is dizzy with success.

Dear God. Pavel's voice is low. We are rich here by comparison. We have both the sea and the land. They will seize my boat?

I don't know.

He finishes the stew by raising the bowl. Filters the bones with his teeth. Sets it down. Feels the other's eye upon him.

Pavel's question is again quietly spoken: Do you work for them?

He turns abruptly. I wish to see her and then I will go. Tomorrow I will go.

You cannot see her. She cannot leave her bed.

Then allow me to sit with her.

I cannot.

We were friends. Let me sit with her awhile.

You caused a great deal of pain.

I am making peace.

Your own peace. None of ours.

You have hidden her away here.

She chooses her life.

A half hour and then I will be gone.

I cannot.

Does she have no say?

Please. Pavel is breathing at the top of his lungs.

Then let me stay tomorrow. I will work.

My son will return tomorrow. You must go. Pavel rises slowly. Do you work for them?

Despite himself, he cannot keep the anger from his voice: Do you think that in a thousand years I would do anything to harm her?

Thank you for your kindness. Try to sleep.

The night hardens into frost and he awakes shivering in his own sweat. The bed dank. His throat thirsty. The glands in his neck swollen. He swings himself up. A pearl rime is climbing the window pane. The sky has lifted. The mountains are clear to their fell heights.

He steps back from the table. Strips. Stands a

moment, shivering hard. Uses the towel that Anna has brought to dry himself as best he can. Then he dresses quickly in the underclothes that he wore on his first day – washed in the river. He puts on his fur jacket. He turns his blankets inside out and lies back down on the edge where the sheet is a little less damp. The shivering is terrible. He cannot sleep. His head hurts whenever he moves. There is nothing to do but lie.

In all the infinite whereabouts of the world, she is here. When so many are forcibly parted, lost to one another, dead, gone, impossible, yet she is here . . . It is another madness then to be shuddering in the darkness on the narrow edge of this wretched bed when he might just as well be in some other land, some forgotten night.

The door is icing shut and he has to push sharply back and forth to open it. He passes outside. And the emptiness of the valley almost overpowers him again. A vast and senseless beauty.

He walks towards the house. His step sounds unwelcome even to his own ears so he treads on the grass by the side of the path.

Inside the little gate, he stops and stares up at the house. There are no lights but a glow in the kitchen from the dying fire. His eyes fix on the lintel where she so often leaned out to see him coming, or wave his going. He guesses the room in which they lay belongs to her children now.

Were it not for fear of her girl discovering him, he wishes that he might set down here, his face to the house, his back to the low stony wall, and pass from consciousness in the coldness of the night. Pavel would bury him well.

His pack is readied. He will go at first light. He presses his knuckles to his forehead. There is nobody to tell, nothing to say or do, but live with all of this in his heart; and then die with it.

V

No knock. But the latch clicks. A figure. Dreaming, not dreaming, he rises.

Stay. No, stay there. Please.

Yelena.

No, please do not get up. I will sit here.

Yelena.

No. I am asking you.

Yelena.

I will sit here. She indicates the chair.

You have come.

Yes.

I did not . . . Yelena, let me look at you. Let me look at you. Let me light the lamp.

No. Please. Stay there. Stay.

He hovers at the very edge of the bed. Are you better? I cannot believe . . .

I am able to get up. As you see, I am able to walk here. The worst of it has passed.

She turns the table chair around and sits facing him. She is dressed in a greatcoat. Her hands deep in the warm dens of the sleeves. She wears boots on her feet, laces untied. Her hair is uncombed and straggled about her shoulders. She appears thinner than he remembers, the sickness perhaps, and her eyes seem the deeper for that. Underneath her coat, she wears some kind of shirt undone at the collar and beneath that a night gown. The moonlight falls in the shape of a diamond on her neck.

Your eye is cut, she says. How did you get here? Tell me that you went around.

I came over.

I was sure so.

I thought you didn't know.

Truly men do not understand women, she says and pauses, as if in other circumstances she might smile. Of course I knew. Anna cannot keep secrets.

And now that she is here in front of him, it seems the maddest thing of all that they did not speak immediately. He leans forward.

How long do we have? Are you—

I promised I would return before the light. Before Anna wakes.

Pavel knows?

Yes. It is the only way.

He shakes his head emphatically, as if grateful for something new and certain to disbelieve.

What kind of a man is he?

He is not like you.

I am sure so.

He is a good man.

I do not believe you told him. He would not have let you come here. How did you leave without waking him?

I asked him to trust me. I promised that you would be gone in the morning.

Must I go?

You are as I remember you, she says.

Too fast, he reaches out his hand for her but she does not take it. Instead she watches him intently as if ready to spring away should he transgress.

Yelena, I am . . . He begins but then falters. Her face is transfixing.

She softens her guard but does not take his hand. I am happy to see you, she says. Now that I do. I thought I would never see you again. I did not know if you were alive – out there in the world. But I am glad that it is so.

His hand falls away though he leans further forward still.

Yelena, I am lost.

She shrinks back from him. I cannot help you.

There is nothing left of me that does not want for you.

Please. No. I cannot say anything. You caused so much pain.

He holds out his palms again, barely resting on the farthest edge of the bed.

You planned the days and the nights I was to come, he says. You wanted to see me. You never once sent me away.

You had a woman. You did not leave her.

You had Pavel.

I was married. I am married. I wear his ring.

We were young. We did not know what it was we were living. We did not know the meaning of anything. We did not know ourselves.

Even then, I was yours for the taking. If only you had found the courage.

Yelena.

Stay there. Please. For me.

But now she touches his extended fingertips with her own.

His voice is a whisper. Lie here with me.

No.

Lie with me.

I cannot.

Lie down with me.

Ivan.

Their fingertips are hooked.

I cannot. I cannot. But here . . . here sit by me. For a moment she is whispering too and they are as they were. Yet immediately she catches herself and speaks as if to organize a card game: Here, sit by me; here. Fetch a chair. We can look out of the window.

In one movement, he rises from the bed, crosses the cabin, lifts out a chair from the confusion by the door and sweeps it down beside her, so that they are sat, side by side at the little table.

He can think of nothing neutral to say.

Your life. Your life here is . . . very happy?

Apart from this sickness. Though Pavel worries. There are more changes coming. I know no other.

Your children are growing.

My life is . . . is as you imagine. I would rather you tell me where your life has taken you. She turns and looks at him. You are sickening – oh, you are such a foolish man – out all day in the rain like a stupid donkey.

Did Anna tell you?

I was watching.

It is warmer where their legs touch though neither had contrived it so. They look out where the window is clear, above the patterns of the frost.

He tries to think of other things to say but it is impossible to talk of anything secondary. He turns to her.

Yelena, I have made a terrible mistake. I do not understand myself. I do not understand my own mind.

She does not look at him but speaks her words clearly, as if to the world outside. You hurt me so deeply that I cannot find my old self again.

I am sorry.

I would have done anything for you.

I do not understand how I can be so much my own enemy . . . It is plain to me that I loved you. That I love you now. That you are love's meaning.

Please . . . please, Ivan, don't talk.

Yelena, I am sorry.

Give me your hand.

Still without looking at him, she lays her palm on the table and he grasps it.

Outside the window, everything seems silver in

the world. The moon. The snow. And the streams like necklaces strewn on the mountainsides.

They are silent awhile then he asks: Do you still go dancing?

Sometimes I do.

The first time I saw you, you were dancing. Even then, my heart stopped every time you left the room and beat faster on your return.

I saw you, too.

You stayed in the village that night.

With my husband's sister.

And the next day, I watched all day from where I was supposed to be working. How I hated that posting only the day before. And how I loved it then because it kept me there. And suddenly you appeared, walking by my window.

A good man would not have followed me. Why did you follow me? Why did you follow me, Ivan?

I could not let you pass my life by. I followed you all the way out of the town. And I thought that you would surely stop there, but you kept on, so I kept on too.

I know. I knew you were following me. You frightened me.

I followed you by the river.

I know.

I followed you to the sea. Miles and miles down that path.

And then you came running up to me as if the whole purpose of your life was to speak to me that very moment.

Yelena, I don't know what to do.

There is nothing to do. I am in your heart. You in mine. That is enough.

How can you say that?

It has to be.

The air is everywhere cold in the room, save for the touch of their hands, their legs, as if urging them in on one another. But the moon is falling behind the mountains.

Leave with me now, he says.

I cannot. Her silent tears seem silver too.
Come with me.
I cannot.
You can.
I cannot.
Yelena.
Don't talk. Hold my hand.
I have fallen from grace.
Hold my hand until the morning.

He walks the track by the shore alone. Sees the boy coming the other way a long time before they meet.

Take good care of your mother, he says. Think of her every day.

The boy nods, uncertain.

He looks intently at the raised face for a moment. Then he walks on.

Self Help

Part One

OCTOBER

'The truth was obscure, too profound and too pure,
To live it you had to explode.'

'Journey Through Dark Heat', BOB DYLAN

Love and Chaos

I

Gabriel Glover

He was relieved to be again among the Russians. Nothing to do with his head, or even his heart, but in his soul: some kind of internal alignment or tessellation. He looked up at the clock on the wall above the brown lift doors. He'd lost two hours with the delays. But the London panic had given way to cool urgency, a calculating haste. There would be the visa and passport queues. There would be the usual wrangle with the taxi driver – unless he agreed up front to pay the tourist price. And then there would be traffic on Moskovsky . . . An hour and a quarter and he should be there.

The doors opened. The other Europeans and the

Americans hesitated. He pushed his way inside with the Russians and a Finnish businessman with a tatty attaché. Everyone was already smoking. He squashed up and breathed it in: the flavour of the tobacco – more aromatic, smokier somehow. An old woman swathed in a heavy black shawl with her hair tied up in a scalp-tightening white bun began shouldering her myriad straps, grasping numberless bags, grimly determined to be the first out.

But he was quicker. He walked swiftly across the vast immigration hall – the high two-tone walls, light Soviet tan at the base and dark Soviet mahogany at the top. There were only two queues for non-residents. He had hoped for three or four. The first was shorter but comprised disorderly families and excited tourists; the second was mainly businessmen, money people. Follow the money. Money, after all, had won.

He put down his bag. These last few miles always seemed such an incremental agony; especially when the previous thousand he had scorched across the curve of the Earth. And now the candour that he had been evading for the last thirty-six hours finally ambushed him: OK, yes, it was true: this call had been different. Much worse. Something was really wrong. Something serious. Otherwise why would he have gone straight to the airport this morning and taken the first flight via Hel-bloody-sinki?

The slab-faced man in the booth looked up from the pages of the passport and met his eyes through the bullet-proof glass.

'Your name?'

'Gabriel Glover.'

'How old are you?'

'Thirty-two.'

There was a long scrutinizing pause, as if the official was formulating a difficult third question, something beginning with 'why'. Gabriel straightened up, consciously pulling his shoulders back, as both Lina and Connie reminded him to do – one thing at least they had in common – and stood with proper posture at his full five eleven. He was dressed half scruffily, in cheap jeans and scuffed boots, and half elegantly, in a dark tailored pure-wool suit jacket and fine white shirt – as though he had not been able to make up his mind about who he really was or which side he was on when he set out. He had the figure of someone thin through restlessness, through exercise of the mind rather than of the body; he had liquid dark eyes and his hair was near black and kicked and kinked at the ends, not so much a style as a lack of one, stylishly passing itself off. Immigration officials usually had him down as Mediterranean before they opened up his passport: Her Britannic Majesty requests and requires . . .

The official's silence was becoming a test of stamina. He felt the urge to say something – any-thing – whatever confession was most required. But at last the Russian gave a grotesque smile fol-lowed by a parody of that long-suffering American imperative: 'Enjoy.'

'Thank you.'

And his passport was returned to him slowly beneath the glass – as if it documented nothing but the transit excuses of a notorious pimp turned pederast turned priest turned politician. (Truly these people were the masters of contempt.) Now he had to wait for his luggage. They had forced him to check it in: too heavy.

For five minutes, he fidgeted by the jaws of the empty carousel like an actor misguidedly aping madness. Then he could stand it no longer. He struck yet another deal with himself – no smoking in London but, OK, fine abroad – and set off to buy some cigarettes from the kiosk with the roubles he had left over from the last trip. When was that? Six weeks ago? No, less . . . Four weeks ago. This had to stop.

There was no relief at first – just acridity and watering eyes – but by midway through the second, he was tempered, smoking greedily and watching the Russians. If ever there was a nation that understood waiting . . . And it occurred to him all over again why she had wanted to come back: because there was something that appealed to her particular vanity here – something fierce and irreducible, some semi-nihilistic condition of character. He remembered her speaking about just this quality when he was a child. She too must have been quite young then, one of the London parties perhaps – he and Isabella, his twin sister, had been allowed to stay up, listening carefully for their cues in the adult conversation. She was talking to Grandpa Max: 'The difference between the Russian character and the Western is that we Russians have learned to live our days in the full knowledge that – whatever transpires in the interim – the sun will eventually expand and humanity will be incinerated. It's a way of life precisely opposite to the American Dream. Call it Russian Fatalism if you like. But it gives us a sense of perspective, a sense of humour and, perhaps, a certain dignity.'

He exhaled smoke through his nose. Her declarations and her pronunciations – was ever a person so convinced of the absolute truth of her latest opinion? She must have been unbearable when she was younger. Her voice was in his head too much these days – especially since the calls had started in earnest; indeed, there were moments when he found himself unable to distinguish his thoughts from hers. His luggage.

'. . . You're just like your father.'

'I'm not listening to this. That's not even true. I've got to go to bed now.'

'You are still with Lina?'

(Lina's voice through the open bedroom door: 'Gabriel? Are you off the phone? Can you bring me some water? And put the lettuce back in the fridge.')

'Since we spoke yesterday?' It was Sunday night. He tried to keep the anger out of his voice. 'Am I still with Lina since this time yesterday? Yeah. Since yesterday, I'm still with Lina. The same as the last four years. Nothing has changed. Listen, I am—'

'And Connie?'

The line clicked irregularly, all the way across Europe.

'Nothing has changed in the last twenty-four hours.' He almost hissed the words. That was unusually devious and unnecessary, even by her standards. 'But you know I can't speak . . .'

'You can always speak to me.'

He had started whispering. 'Lina is awake. It's . . . It's midnight. I have to go to bed.'

'Going sideways, going sideways, going sideways. Can't go forward. Can't go back. So you go sideways.'

'I'll call tomorrow from work.'

'Like your father.'

'No. Stop. That's it. I'll call you tom—'

'Don't go.'

Her voice contained a new note of . . . of what? Desperation?

'I promise I will call you tomorrow.'

'Gabriel.'

He felt her reaching in for his heart. And he felt his heart uncoil. 'OK. But I do have to go soon. And – and you should be in bed, too. It's what? Christ, it's past three with you. It's the middle of the night.'

'It's difficult for you. I know.'

'What is? You're not sounding great. You're rasping. Seriously, is everything OK?'

'To inhabit yourself fully. Very few people do this anymore. But you and I, we try – correct? We try to hold the line . . . Even though this will cost us almost everything we have – this great indignity, this great antagonism, this great protest.' She coughed. 'Which is itself pointless.'

Unnerved now. More riddles. His attention wholly focused.

'But – listen to me.' She spoke more steadily. 'You have to be fierce in the face of all the cowardice you see around you. And you have to say:

"No. For me: no. I will not. I will not lie down and I will not give up. I will not do, or be, or become anything that you wish me to. However you disguise it, however you describe it – politics, religion, economics – I will continue to stand here and tell you that what you believe in is a lie and what you have become is a falsehood.'"

'Why – why – are you talking to me like this?'

Another cough and suddenly she became urgent: 'Will you come tomorrow?'

'To Petersburg?'

'Yes.'

'I can't. I'm at work tomorrow.'

'Your work is a joke. Come tomorrow.'

'I can't just . . . Why are you laughing? Jesus – you're coughing.' He continued to speak but he knew that she could not hear. 'Oh God . . . It's getting worse.'

For nearly a minute he stood there, listening to her hacking. But it was unendurable. So he started up again, shouting into the phone, regardless of waking Lina: 'Can you hear me? Are you there? Hold the phone up.' A few seconds' quiet – her breathing like wind through rusted barbed wire. 'Oh God . . . you're crying.'

And then this: 'Do you love me, Gabriel?'

She had never asked him such a thing. Not once.

'Yes. Of course. You know I do.'

'Say it in Russian.'

'Ya tyebya lyublyu.'

'Come tomorrow. Promise me.'

'You've got to move back to London. And you don't have to live in the old house.' He would have set out that instant if he could have made it there any faster by doing so.

'Petersburg is my home. You must be here tomorrow. I will give you the money. I want to see you. I will talk. There are so many things I have to tell you.'

'I need a visa.'

'Come the day after, then. Get an express visa. I'll pay.'

'Are you crying?'

'Promise me.'

'OK. OK. I promise.'

It was one thirty-five UK time when he finally hung up. Three and a half hours later, he was standing at the front of the already-lengthening queue outside the Russian Embassy on Kensington Palace Gardens, watching a grout-grey dawn seep slowly through the cracks in the east.

The driver was crazier than he had dared hope. He clasped the handrail above the passenger door, the muscles tensing in his upper arm as the taxi veered left onto Moskovsky – wide and straight, the road into town was as Stalin-soaked in the monochrome of tyranny as the centre of the city was bright and colourful with the light of eighteenth-century autocracy.

'Democracy is difficult for us, Gabriel,' she

often said. 'In Russia we are required to live within the pathologies of the strongest man – whatever he titles himself. That way we all know where we are and what we are doing. However bad it gets.'

The cars were moving freely – the battered Czech wrecks and tattered Russian rust-crates, the sleek German saloons and the tinted American SUVs, overtaking, undertaking, switching lanes in a fat salsa of metal and gasoline. Still no phone network; it didn't usually take this long. He shifted in the back seat, lit his fourth cigarette and wound down the window as the cab slowed for the lights. A mortally decrepit bus bullied its way across the intersection discharging plumes of what looked like . . . like coal dust. The pollution was worsening: particles hung heavy and brazen as nails in the lower air – a blunt parody of the fine mists that must have once come dancing up the Neva in from the sea to greet great Peter himself as he rode out across the marshes to meet his enemies.

He would stay with the cab: twenty minutes

and he'd be there. No need to jump out and take the underground. Gorolov-Geroev Park was just ahead now – he could see the scrub-trees behind the tarnished railings and there was the crooked-nosed old man with that same heavily lapelled sports jacket still selling books and magazines on the corner. Not really selling. More like minding them for someone or something never to come. Jesus, it was as if he had not been away. How many times was he going to have to do this?

He bent to look up. The sky was low and louring. The plane had been in rain clouds for much of the descent. The wind must be carrying them inland from the west. He tried to listen to the music from the ill-tuned station on the car radio; it sounded like Kino. Something off Gruppa Krovi maybe – he couldn't be sure – beauty and despair bound in razor wire and thrown overboard together, white-lipped now beneath the ice, thrashing it out, life and death. His sister would have known the exact song, the exact version. A current of anger joined the stream of his thinking. Isabella hadn't been over for nearly a year. Longer, in fact; twenty-one months – Christmas – the Mariinsky – that vicious wind on the walk home, which froze the nose and iced the eyeballs, three atheists on their knees at Kazan Cathedral early the next morning.

The truth was that he wished he had managed to get hold of Isabella last night instead of leaving a message. The truth was that he was no longer sure of the truth. And he trusted his sister to apprehend things precisely – to seek out the quiddity of things and once grasped never to let go, to insist, to assert, to confirm. Whereas for him . . . For him the truth seemed to be slipping away with each passing year – losing distinctiveness, losing clarity, losing weight. Duplicity, hypocrisy and cant, the primary colours he once would have scorned, he now saw in softer shades. Perhaps this was the ageing process: bit by bit truth grows faint until she vanishes completely leaving you stranded on the path, required to choose a replacement guide from those few stragglers left among your party – surly prejudice, grinning bewilderment, purblind grievance. The thin beep of his phone locating a network.

He sat up smartly, let the cigarette fall outside the window and pressed the last-dial button. A child's unmediated eagerness ran through him. With every second he expected her voice . . . But the ringing continued as if to spite him. And he began to picture the phone shrilling on the side table by the bay window – the dusty light, the red-cushioned casement seats, the chess set forever ready for action. He imagined her climbing from the bath, or hurrying from the shower, or fumbling with keys and bags at the door.

Eventually, the line went dead.

He hit redial. They were coming towards Moskovskaya – he could see the statue of Lenin a little further on the right arm aloft, one of the few still standing. This time he listened intently to the exact pitch and interval of the ring tone. No answer. No bloody answer.

The line went dead again. She must be out. Maybe she was tired of waiting and he'd get there to find one of her notes on the table: 'At cafe such and such with so and so, come and join' – as if he should know the cafe or the friend. Or maybe she was just refusing to pick up the phone for reasons she would soon be telling him – something dark and colossally unlikely involving organized crime, her time in the Secretariat. Redial. The fact was that he was utterly at a loss as to what she was really trying to communicate to him. The direct accusations, sly allusions, subject swerves, sudden changes of register that served (and were meant to serve) only to draw further attention to the preceding hints. Redial. Individual exchanges made sense and yet when he got off the phone he could not discern what lay behind her pointed choice of subject, her denouncements, her fabrications. He gave up as the line went dead the fourth time.

Why wasn't she answering the bloody phone? And suddenly, all his anger passed away. And he knew that he would do this forever if necessary.

His mobile had heated his ear and he put it down on the seat away from him as the driver slowed for the traffic again. And here they were crawling beneath mighty Lenin's arm. 'That failure,' she always said, 'is our failure, Gabriel, is the failure of all of us. Such dreams expired. More dreams than we can imagine – all extinguished by that failure. Not just in the past but in the future too: and that's the real sadness, the real tragedy. We have – all of us – the whole world – we have all of us lost our belief in our better selves. And the great told-you-so of capitalism will roll out across the earth until there is no hiding place. And every day that passes, Marx will be proved more emphatically right. And every man or woman waking in the winter to the slavery of their wages will know it in their heart.'

*

He stood for an anxious moment by the iron railings of the canal embankment, putting away his wallet and glancing up at the second-floor balcony. The tall windows were closed. But the curtains were not drawn. The driver struggled with the lock of the buckled boot, the gusting wind causing his jacket to billow. Rain was coming. Gabriel could smell the damp in the air. He took his bag and hurried across the street.

He reached the gates that blocked his way to the courtyard – like most in the old part of town, the flats were accessed off the various staircases within. And only now he remembered the need to punch in the security code. What was the number? He couldn't recall. He pressed the buzzer and waited. Maybe she had been in the bath when he rang. Or maybe her phone wasn't working. He simply hadn't thought about this. He'd assumed she would be home. And if, by some strange chance, not, then he had all the keys to let himself in . . . but the security code. No. He'd forgotten all about the bloody security code.

He tried a few combinations at random. He jabbed at her buzzer repeatedly. Nothing happened. And there was no voice from the intercom. The first twist of rain came and he leaned in to the gate to get beneath the shallow arch. Water began to drip on his bag. Maybe he could try one of the other buzzers and explain . . . But even if they spoke English – unlikely – there was no way on earth they'd let him in; crime had seen to that. He pressed her buzzer again. He did not know what else to do.

No answer.

Abruptly, the full force of his panic returned – a tightening in his throat, a clamping of his teeth at the back of his jaw, the sound of his own blood coursing in his ears. (The fear – yes, that was what it was – the fear in her voice on the telephone.) He looked around – face taut now – hoping for a car or another resident approaching. Someone to open the gate. Where was everybody? The whole of the city had vanished. This was insane. Over on the other side of the canal, two men were sprinting for shelter. They ducked down the stairs into the opposite cafe.

Yana. Of course. Yana would know the code. Yana's mother was in and out all the time – cleaning officially, though mainly consuming expensive tea and gossiping. Oh please Christ Yana's working today. He picked up his bag and dashed across the bridge. The Kokushkin Bridge on which poor Rodya stared into the murky water to contemplate his crime, Gabriel, can you imagine it?

He was across. He dived down the cafe stairs – slipped on the wet stone and nearly fell, reaching out for the door to stop himself and somehow bloodying his knuckle as he crashed inside. But he cared nothing for the eyes that were on him as he walked over to the bar cursing under his breath.

'Is Yana here? Do you speak English?'

'Yes, I do.' The girl at the bar had a staff T-shirt: 'CCCP Cafe: The Party People'.

'Is Yana here? Yana.'

'Yes. She is. What d—'

'Can you get her?' He had not seen this girl before; he tried to ameliorate his manner but to little effect. 'Sorry. I'm sorry. Can you tell her Gabriel is here? It's about Maria – she'll know.'

'OK.' The girl had registered his urgency and locked the till as quickly as she could. 'Please. Wait here.'

'Yes. I'll wait.' He glanced at the walls, which were pasted in lacquered old editions of *Pravda* – Khrushchev kissing a dead astronaut's son, Andropov, Old Joe himself – always a shock to see that, yes, he was a person of flesh and blood and conversation – leaning forward to say something to the woman seated beside his driver as the state car processed down Nevsky Prospekt. How many times had he and Isabella tried to read these walls and recreate in their minds what it must have been—

'Gabe. Hi. Hello. How are you? I did not know

you were coming back. Katja says you are a man who lost it.'

'Sorry. Yana, I'm just – I can't get in.' He raised his thumb to indicate behind himself. 'What's the combination? The security gate. Do you know it?'

'Yes, of course.' She told him the number, becoming conscious of the alarm in his eyes. 'Is everything OK? How long you here? I didn't know you were coming back. It's lucky you came today, though – I am going to Kiev tomorrow. I have to—'

'It's a flying visit.' He interrupted her. 'I just got in. But I'll be back later. Promise.' He was already turning for the door. 'We'll go out. Definitely. You can tell me about what is really happening – the news isn't clear.'

The rain had soused the cobbles but this time he crossed the bridge at a flat sprint, all the while keeping his eyes on the window above the balcony. Nobody paid him any attention – the random autumn flurries of wet weather that came squalling in off the Gulf of Finland often caused old and young alike to scurry and dash. A woman holding a magazine above her head left the shelter of the hairdresser's canopy and scuttled to her car door.

He was back at the security gate. He pressed in the numbers. The metal doors began to swing open jerkily: a moment to marvel at how the simple fact of his knowing the right combination was all the difference and then he was through, into the courtyard.

The rain was slicking his hair on to his forehead and causing him to blink. The cars within looked more numerous than the last time. He was unashamedly thinking with her voice now: There you go: capitalism's pubescent little triumphs on every hand, see how they vaunt it. Water was gushing down the side of the building where the guttering was broken. His mind would not bend to. But his heart was pestling itself mad against the mortar of the present: suffering now from some inarticulate dread – a terrifying feeling that came at him as he reached the staircase in the corner of the quadrangle, grinding his very quick to powder.

The stench of cat urine assailed him, slowed him, as he hit the stairs. She was a little demented, perhaps. Admit it. That's why he couldn't get at what she meant, what she was really saying to him. She contradicted herself twelve times a day, twelve times an hour, and who can believe someone who . . . Distraction, though, distraction, he breathed: back to now, back. Up we go. Up we go. Why wasn't he running anymore? Maybe she was refusing to answer the entryphone on purpose. And the telephone. In two minutes, she would be taking her perverse Petersburg pleasure in telling him how the criminal gangs were now calling door to door in the afternoons in the hope of being admitted without the need for time-consuming breaking-and-entering procedures. It's not as bad as Moscow, but it's very dangerous sometimes here, Gabriel. And there was another murder just over in Sennaya . . . He turned to take the third flight. The seconds were stalling. He noticed details he had never noticed before. The filth and the smell, the colours, the lack of colours, the chipped and broken sad stone stairs, the million cigarette butts underfoot, the unconcealed pipes all caked thick with dust and grime forever wheezing and choking up and down and back and across the stairwell, the metal-slabbed apartment doors riveted with legion bolts and locks and tarnished somehow – despite the steel – by nameless cats or poisonous leaks or dogs or rats . . . Her thick exterior padlock was undone.

So she must be in.

She must be in – because there was no possibility that she'd leave that padlock undone if she had gone out. She must be in. But he turned his key and entered the apartment in silence because he could not bring himself to call her name.

The light was dim. The wooden floor smelled of polish. He stepped onto the narrow carpet that ran down the centre of the hall. And now he had stopped moving altogether. The familiar pictures – his father in Paris in 1968, Isabella in New York, the Highgate house, his father on the telephone with a cigarette, Nicholas II and his family, him and his sister as babies in a pram, some famous clown white-faced in Red Square, the map of Europe stained with the brown ring mark of a wine glass over the Balkans, the icons, especially the bloody icons . . . These familiar pictures seemed suddenly remote, alien, unconnected with him – as though he had wandered into the flat of a vanished stranger whose life he must untangle.

Someone dropped something in the apartment above. He let his bag fall and ran, left, towards her bedroom. The door was open. The heavy curtains drawn. Her books piled untidily on the floor by her fallen lamp. Flowers thirsty in the vase. Her favourite shawl strewn across the floor by the chest. A full mug of black tea by the bed. Pills. The piano. The bed itself empty. He ran back down the corridor, pushing doors as he went – bathroom, kitchen, study . . . But he slowed on the threshold of the last, the drawing room – as she called it, high ceilings, grand, with my tall windows for the White Nights, Gabriel, for the cool air in the summer, for the best view in all of Petersburg where our history is made.

His mother was lying on the floor by the desk. He was on his knees and by her side in an instant. Her eyes were open but shrouded somehow in a shimmering film of reflected light. And when he called her name out loud at last and raised her up, her body was cold and slight. And she seemed to have shrunk, to be falling down – down into herself, down into the floor, seeking the earth. And there was neither voice nor breath from her lips.